To the Rescue!

POLICE CARS

By Lois Fortuna

Gareth Stevens
PUBLISHING

Please visit our website, www.garethstevens.com. For a free color catalog of all our high-quality books, call toll free 1-800-542-2595 or fax 1-877-542-2596.

Cataloging-in-Publication Data

Names: Fortuna, Lois.
Title: Police cars / Lois Fortuna.
Description: New York : Gareth Stevens Publishing, 2017. | Series: To the rescue! | Includes index.
Identifiers: ISBN 9781482452020 (pbk.) | ISBN 9781482446616 (library bound) | ISBN 9781482446500 (6 pack)
Subjects: LCSH: Police vehicles–Juvenile literature.
Classification: LCC HV7936.V4 F67 2017 | DDC 629.225–dc23

First Edition

Published in 2017 by
Gareth Stevens Publishing
111 East 14th Street, Suite 349
New York, NY 10003

Editor: Ryan Nagelhout
Designer: Laura Bowen

Photo credits: Cover, p. 1 Charlie Hutton/Shutterstock.com; p. 5 © iStockphoto.com/kali9; p. 7 © iStockphoto.com/Mie Ahmt; p. 9 (top left, top right) Leonard Zhukovsky/Shutterstock.com; p. 9 (middle left) Dschwen/Wikimedia Commons; p. 9 (middle right) mikecphoto/Shutterstock.com; p. 9 (bottom left) Kaesler Media/Shutterstock.com; p. 9 (bottom right) IFCAR/Wikimedia Commons; pp. 11, 24 (computer) Thinkstock/Stockbyte/Getty Images; p. 13 KYTan/Shutterstock.com; pp. 15, 24 (radio) Hill Street Studios/Blend Images/Getty Images; pp. 17, 24 (lights) SergeyIT/Shutterstock.com; p. 19 ksb/Shutterstock.com; p. 21 Anne Kitzman/Shutterstock.com; p. 23 John Roman Images/Shutterstock.com.

Printed in the United States of America

CPSIA compliance information: Batch #CS16GS: For further information contact Gareth Stevens, New York, New York at 1-800-542-2595.

Contents

The police keep us safe.

POLICE
DEPT.

They have their
own cars!

POLICE DEPT.
TO PROTECT AND SERVE
POLICE

Police cars are
many colors.

POLICE DEPARTMENT
CITY OF NEW YORK
NYPD
HYBRID

SHERIFF
KEEPING THE PEACE SINCE 1850

STATE
CAPITOL
POLICE

POLICE

PORT AUTHORITY
POLICE
NEW YORK
NEW JERSEY
POLICE

PRINCE WILLIAM COUNTY
POLICE

They have a computer.

They have a radio, too.

MEM
PWR OFF
STEP/
SCAN
DISTRESS
MENU
CLR

Police use the radio to talk.

Police cars have
bright lights.
They are red and blue.

Most police cars
are called patrol cars.

HIGHWAY PATROL

Some stop cars
that drive too fast.

POLICE

Other cars are
for dogs!
These are K9 cars.

K-9
KEEP AWAY
POLICE DOG
K9

Words to Know

computer

lights

radio

Index